DINOSNORES

by **Kelly DiPucchio**

illustrated by **Ponder Goembel**

HarperCollinsPublishers

Dinosnores

Text copyright © 2005 by Kelly DiPucchio
Illustrations copyright © 2005 by Ponder Goembel
Manufactured in China.

For information address HarperCollins Children's Books.
a division of HarperCollins Publishers.
1350 Avenue of the Americas. New York. NY 10019.
www.harperchildrens.com

Library of Congress Cataloging-in-Publication Data
DiPucchio. Kelly S.   Dinosnores / by Kelly S. DiPucchio :
illustrated by Ponder Goembel.— 1st ed.   p. cm.
Summary: Relates the earth-changing consequences of
millions of nights of raucous snoring by sleeping dinosaurs.
ISBN 0-06-051577-5 — ISBN 0-06-051578-3 (lib. bdg.)
[1. Dinosaurs—Fiction. 2. Snoring—Fiction. 3. Sound—Fiction.
4. Continents—Fiction. 5. Stories in rhyme.] I. Goembel. Ponder. ill.
II. Title.   PZ8.3.D5998Di 2005   2004004441   [E]—dc22

Typography by Carla Weise
1 2 3 4 5 6 7 8 9 10
❖
First Edition

To all of my T-Rific nieces and nephews:
Katelyn, Kristen, Josh, Rebecca, Rachel,
Sarah, Michael, and Julia
—K.D.

To my brothers, Philip and Luke,
who knew every kind of dinosaur
—P.G.

On a supercontinent,
many million years ago,
dinosaurs prepared for sleep
on cozy lava flows.

They bathed, and brushed, and fluffed their ferns
around the dino site . . .
then laid their horns and spikes to rest
and kissed their eggs good night.

Reptilian birds and dragonflies
drifted through the skies,
while prehistoric crickets sang
Jurassic lullabies.

Soon the peaceful world was rocked,
shaken to its shores . . .
from snouts of sleeping dinosaurs
boomed mammoth dinosnores!

There were

BRONTO-BOOMS,

TRICERA-CRIES,

RAPTOR-RUMBLES,

STEGO-SIGHS...

PROTO-GRUNTS,

DIPLO-HOOTS,

ALLO-SNORTS,

and

TYRANNO-TOOTS!

While dinos slept, winged lizards leapt,
and mammals ran to hide.
Palm trees quivered. Hot springs shivered.
Bugs were petrified!

Still, sleepy rumbling kept on coming
from that dino chorus.
Whistles, grunts, and snorts galore
sprang from every 'saurus!

Their nasal breeze stirred up the seas
and wind storms full of sand.
Swamps and rivers sloshed about . . .
tossed creatures onto land.

That rumpus triggered tremors
and a powerful earthquake.
The shaking scared amphibians
and drove them from the lake.

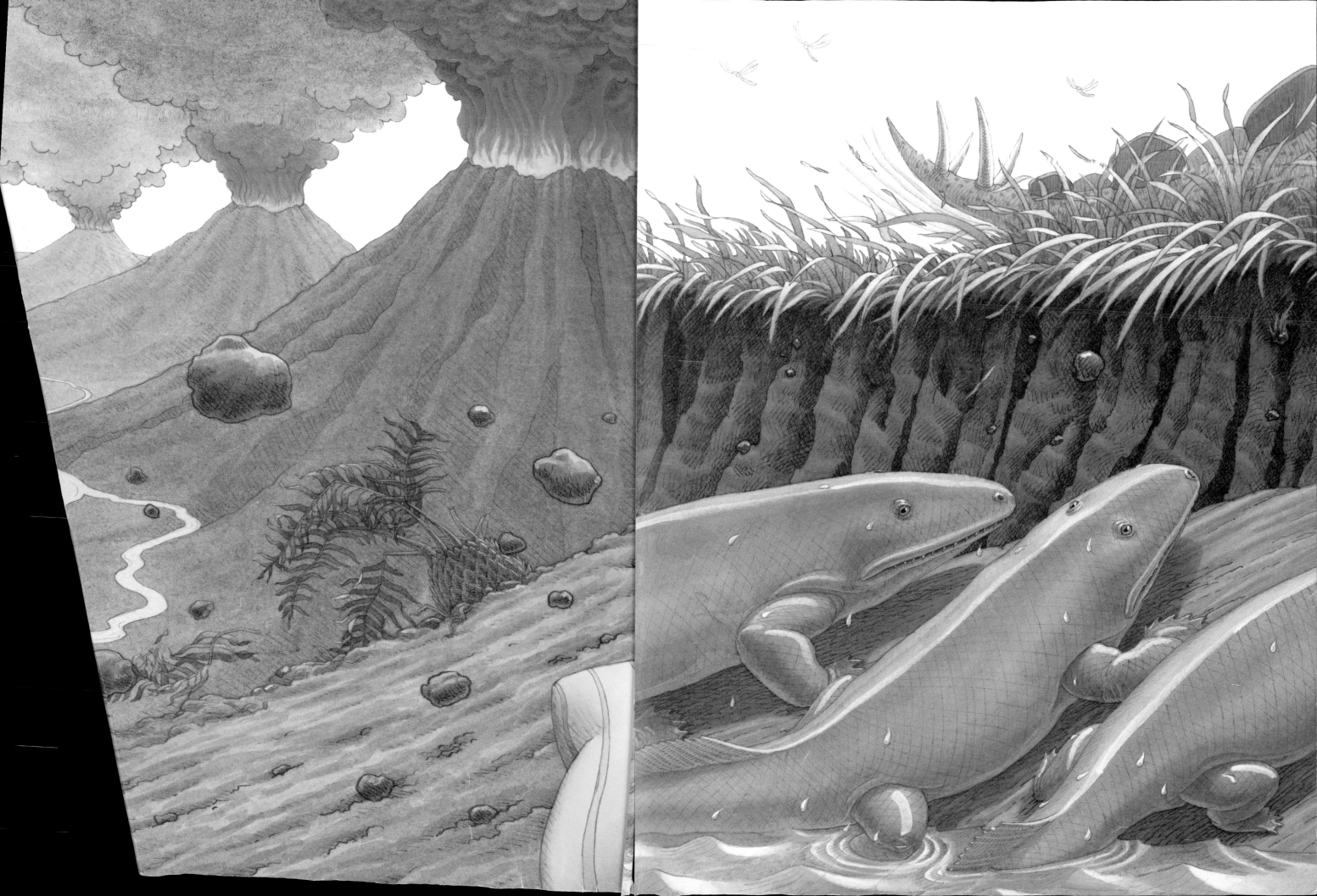

Dino drools made swimming pools
and gooey, slick mudslides.
Sharks and ancient giant squids
surfed slimy spit riptides.

Deep grumbles made rocks tumble
and loud Cretaceous booms!
Chains of sleeping mountain tops
awoke in fiery plumes.

After several million nights like this
of snoring from the pit,
the shaken supercontinent
began to crack and split!

The dinos waved good-bye to friends
and drifted off to sea.
As for the rest, you may have guessed . . .

It's
ancient
history.

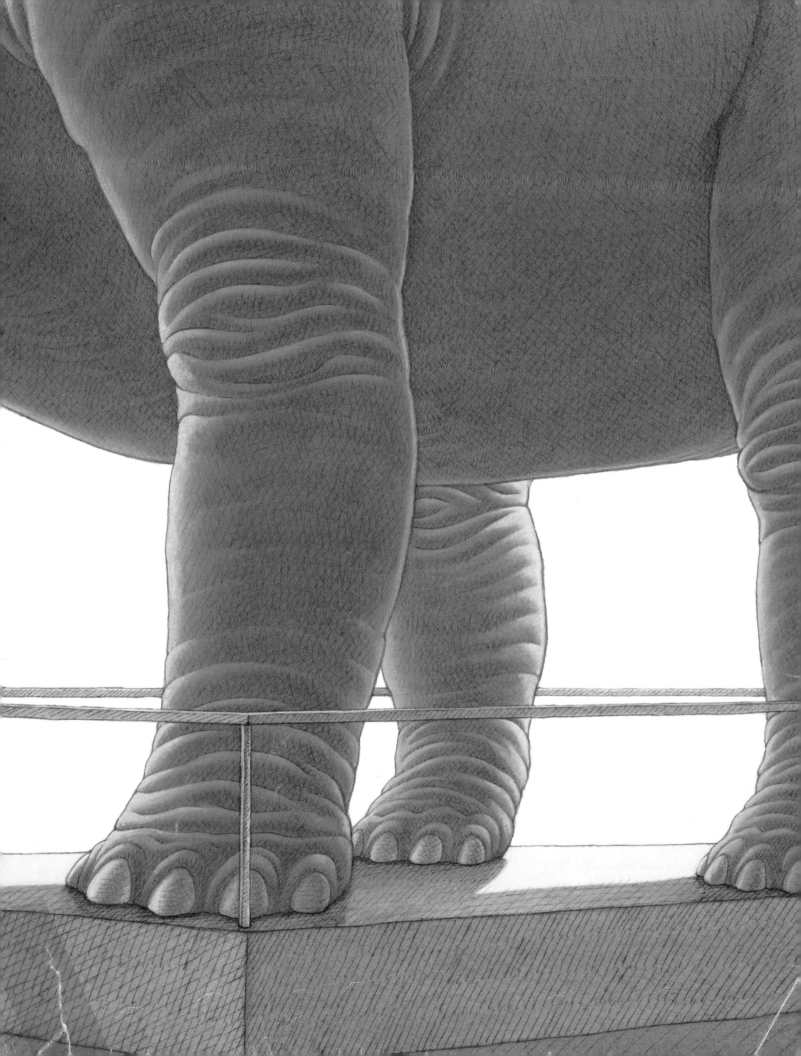

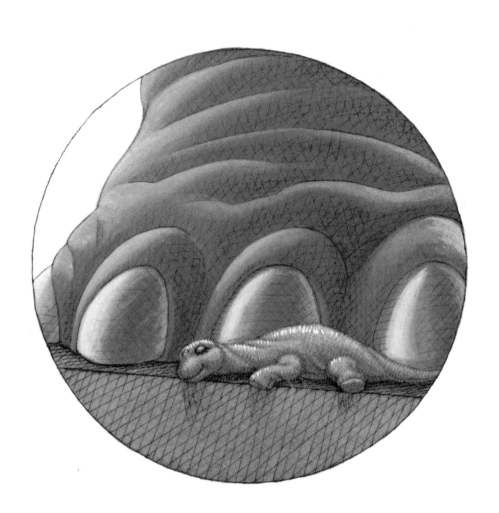